WEST CHICAGO PUBLIC LIBRARY DISTRICT

3 6653 00236 7286

4/14

W9-BAH-502

West Chicago Public Library District
118 West Washington
West Chicago, IL 60185-2803
Phone # (630) 231-1552
Fax # (630) 231-1709

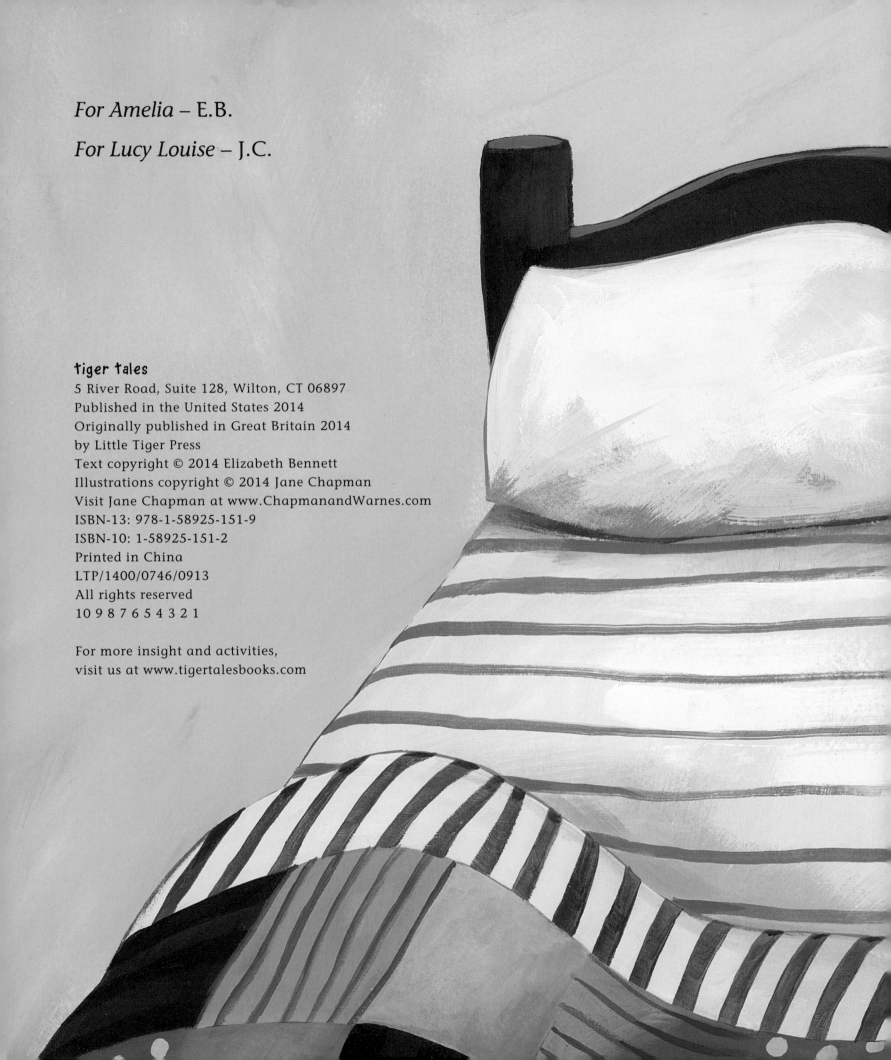

For Amelia – E.B.

For Lucy Louise – J.C.

tiger tales
5 River Road, Suite 128, Wilton, CT 06897
Published in the United States 2014
Originally published in Great Britain 2014
by Little Tiger Press
Text copyright © 2014 Elizabeth Bennett
Illustrations copyright © 2014 Jane Chapman
Visit Jane Chapman at www.ChapmanandWarnes.com
ISBN-13: 978-1-58925-151-9
ISBN-10: 1-58925-151-2
Printed in China
LTP/1400/0746/0913
All rights reserved
10 9 8 7 6 5 4 3 2 1

For more insight and activities,
visit us at www.tigertalesbooks.com

by Elizabeth Bennett

Illustrated by
Jane Chapman

Big

and Small

tiger tales

On a bright and sunny day, Big and Small go out to play.

Big

climbs high.

Small crawls low.

When suddenly, Small stubs his toe.

They cross a stream.
Jump, skip, hop, hop.

When suddenly,
Small has to stop.

"A little help, please!"
calls Small.

What's for lunch? Hmmmmmmm Let's see . . . . .

When suddenly,
Small spots a bee!
"A little help, please!"
calls Small.

Up on a

hill. What fun! Let's roll.

When **suddenly**,
Small's **down**
a hole.
"A little **help**, please!"
calls Small.

Back

home to bed.

They're warm and snug.
But **Big** can't sleep—
he needs a **hug**.
"A little help, please!"
calls **Big**.

Zzzzzzzzzz

zzzzzzzzz